WRONGWAY SANTA

STORY BY
RAE OETTING

DESIGNED AND ILLUSTRATED BY
ART SHARDIN

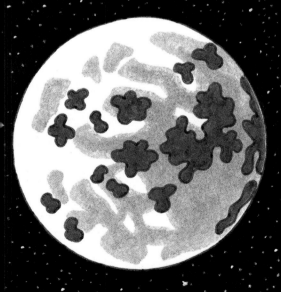

published by

ODDO PUBLISHING
Fayetteville, Georgia

Symbol for exciting book ideas

Read, Explore, and Develop

Library of Congress Catalog Number 90-062546
ISBN 0-87783-254-4

Printed in the United States of America

Of all the tales told
    of old Santa Claus,
Perhaps no other
    can better give pause

Than the time that his wife,
    with love and good will,
Fed each waiting reindeer
    the wrong vitamin pill.

It happened one night,
    before Christmas day,
As Santa rechecked
    and made sure of his way,

On a cold, snowy night
    in the deer-feeding shed
Where the reindeer stood ready
    for the gift-laden sled.

As each elf fine tuned
    and examined the toys,
To make them just right
    for good girls and boys,

She'd given them hay,
  and a measure of oats,
And eight pails of water
  to moisten their throats.

Then suddenly putting
  her head to one side,
She said, "Poor dears,
  you've such a long ride.

"I have some wonderful
  pills you can take.
They'll give your feet wings.
  They'll lessen your ache."

She took from a medicine
   chest on a wall,
A bottle so squat,
   and a bottle so tall.

She set the two bottles
   nearby on a table
And reached for her glasses
   to study each label.

But trying to read
   in a light poor and dim,
She made a mistake
   that was ghastly and grim,

For the bottle she chose
   was the small squatty one,
Marked *Outer Space Flight
On A Super Speed Run!*

She went to the head
   of each deer in its stall.
From the bottle so squat
   she *vitamined* all.

When Santa appeared
    rosy-suited and bright,
He mentioned, "The reindeer
    seem restless tonight.

"No doubt they're just eager,
    as I am, to fly.
But first one last check,
    before we say 'bye.

"Is everything packed?
    Now let's see, my dear,
I'll be wanting my pipe
    and hot cider near,

"And my *just in case kit*
    in the bag, red and white,
Marked *For Emergencies Only*
    On Christmas Eve Night!"

"Yes," Mrs. Claus said,
      "they're all in your grip.
Now be careful, Kris,
      and have a nice trip."

Santa sprang to the sleigh
      to adjust the control
On the board with the knobs
      under *Take-Off, North Pole.*

But his fingers could grasp
      not a single switch
For the sleigh began rolling
      and started to pitch.

As Santa hung on,
    it was all he could do
To keep in his seat
    while the sleigh wildly flew

Behind runaway deer
    filled with outer space pep,
That galloped, careened,
    and gee-hawed out of step.

They swung through the sky
with their gift-laden carrier
So fast that they shattered
the sonic sound barrier.

They broke up the wavelengths,
 they bent the light years,
While all that poor Santa
 could see through his tears

Were the rumps of his reindeer
away up ahead,
And the reins that were hooked
to the front of his sled.

"I've got to do something
to stop this mad flight
For everywhere children
await me tonight!

"My *just in case kit*
      has some magical pills
Just in case while I'm flying
      my reindeer get ill.

"If I can get one
      such pill down the throat
Of each of my reindeer,
      it's a sure antidote."

He took a deep breath
      for he had but one way!
Then carefully Santa
      crawled out of his sleigh.

And as he climbed out
      he held tightly the reins,
For his overweight problem
      provoked a few pains,

While jumbled up wavelengths
  on earth down below
Caused gallery paintings
  that hung in a row,

To shake and to shimmy
  and simply confound
All the people who saw
  this strangeness abound.

They stared in great wonder
  as Blue Boy turned red
And Whistler's Mother
  now stood on her head!

TV sponsors were screaming
  and tearing their hair
For the mixed-up commercials
  that went on the air!

The newest was soap,
  now called *Tell-Tale Gray*,
And the latest in toothpastes
  was *Instant Decay!*

The beaches down south
    in the height of the season,
Were covered with snow,
    and were all out of reason.

The children up north
    threw their scarves to the ground
And stood in the shade
    when they suddenly found

The heat from the south
    that invaded their mountains
Was turning their snowmen
    to high-spouting fountains.

Perhaps the most mixed-up
    event that occurred —
The cat chased the dog —
    both chased by a bird!

Poor Santa saw this
   and he started to plead,
"I've got to reach Dancer.
   He's the one in the lead."

He struggled again
   on the reins he was gripping,
But the harder he tried,
   the more he kept slipping,

Until with a snap
   and a plunge down in space,
The reins that he clung to
   broke loose from the place

Where they first had been fastened
    up tight on the sleigh,
And left poor old Santa
    to dangle and sway.

He swung back and forth,
    he swung side to side,
With no way to slow up
    his runaway ride!

The sleigh up above
   gave a jerk and a lurch
And spilled out some presents
   that fell on a church

Where children were singing
   outside in the snow,
Their voices all blended,
   their faces aglow.

"Oh, dear!" said poor Santa.
     "I surely am troubled.
If I ever get started
     my work will be doubled!

"But first I must stop
     those eight runaway deer.
'Though just how to do it
     is not very clear.

"Perhaps if I swung
   back and forth like a swing,
I could pump myself up,
   I could grab the check rein

"That's fastened up front
   to the sleigh bells on Dancer,
And threads through the rings
   of the bridle on Prancer."

He pumped and he swung
   and he swung and he pumped.
His head was drawn in
   and his shoulders were humped.

He couldn't quite swing
high enough to the side
To grab the check rein
and to stop his wild ride.

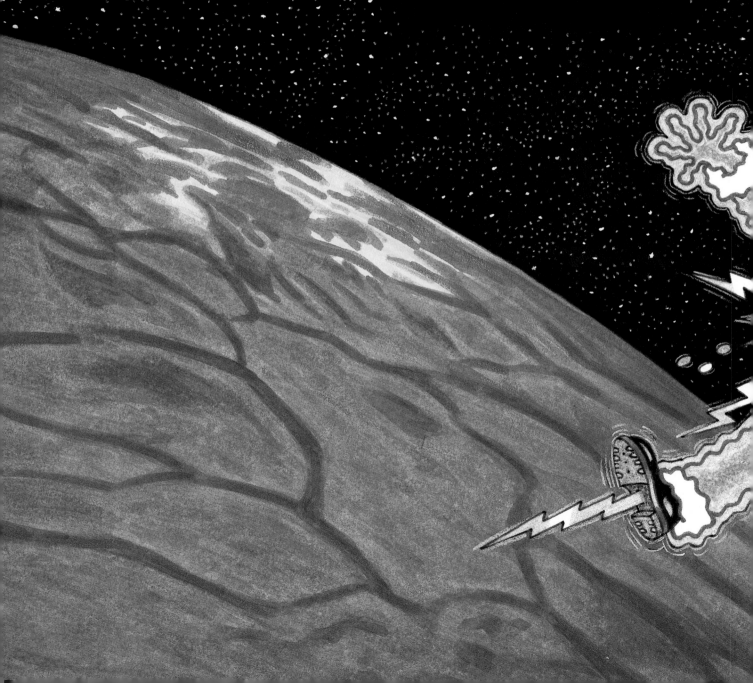

He'd never have made it,
 but when nearing Mars,
He noted some stylishly
 blue-suited stars.

He reached for the nearest.
 He took quite a chance
In grabbing a star
 by the leg of its pants.

Poor Santa Claus shrieked,
   then he leapt a foot higher,
For the star's stylish pants
   were made of blue fire!

The boost that he got
  swung him high into space,
And he sailed through the air
  at a breathtaking pace.

With a plop and a whoosh
  and a resounding smack,
He landed astride
  racing Dancer's brown back.

He caught the check rein,
   slowed his furious ride,
And put the big sleigh
   in a swift downward glide.

"Whoa, you fellows, Whoa!
   Steady there boys!
You're spoiling my ride,
   you're spilling my toys!

"You've upset the earth.
   You've caused quite a fright!
You'll have to slow down
   just to set things aright!"

KAWBAM!!!

He brought the deer team
    to a halt on a hill
And quickly gave each
    a magical pill.

Then back in his sleigh
    Santa looked at his list.
"I must hurry all night
    so no child will be missed."

As he slid across roofs
    with his well-loaded pack,
He was happy to note
    the old earth settling back.

He saw Whistler's Mother
    again in her chair,
And heard old commercials
    extolling their fare.

Children up north put
    their warm coats back on,
While down in the south
    the cold air was all gone.

And the beautiful carols
    of Christmastime
Again warmed the heart
    like the bells of a chime.

When Santa had made
    all the stops on his route,
And got the spilled presents
    somehow straightened out,

He headed for home
    as the new dawn was breaking,
With an empty gift sleigh
    and a back that was aching.

He drove to the deer shed
and saw with surprise
Mrs. Claus standing there
with tears in her eyes.

He brought the eight deer
to a trembling standstill,
Then jumped from the sleigh
and asked, "Are you ill?"

"No, I'm not really ill,"
Mrs. Claus shook her head,
"But I worried for fear
you'd be sleigh-wrecked or dead!

"I made a mistake.
I misread the label
On the bottle so squat
that stood on the table.

"I wanted some vitamin
    pills for the deer,
But the bottle I chose
    held space pills, I fear.

"I have worried all night.
    I have not been to bed
Since I made that mistake
    in the deer-feeding shed."

Then Santa Claus took
    Mrs. Claus by the arm.
"My love," he said gently,
    "I came to no harm.

"It's true that my deer
    headed out into space
In a wrong-way direction,
    at a superfast pace.

"I had quite a time
    near a planet called Mars
Where I made the acquaintance
    of blue-suited stars.

"In fact, you might say,
    that my sleigh ride tonight
Was standard enough
    for an outer space flight.

"But for an old-fashioned Santa
    this outer space flight
Was a little too taxing
    for a Christmas Eve night.

"My weary old bones
    need a normal night's rest,
And a normal sleigh ride
    next year will be best!"

about the author

RAE OETTING's productive career long identified her with North America's great wilderness. Complemented by her talents for writing and photography, Rae was able to convey her deep appreciation for the outdoors to all readers — adults and children alike.

As a long-time member of the Outdoor Writers of America Association, Rae travelled frequently throughout North America gathering material for the many articles she authored on sports, fishing, and travel. Her stories appeared in *Field and Stream*, *Travel*, *Southern Living*, *Saskatchewan Fish and Game*, *Great Lakes Sportsman*, *Snow Goer*, and many others. She wrote a weekly column for three newspapers and was camping editor of Jim Peterson's *Outdoor News*.

Rae was also a member of the Sunshine City Camera Club of St. Petersburg, Florida. Her flair with the camera won several awards for her photographic works.

An accomplished educator, Rae taught numerous courses including, *Writing for Publication* in the Minneapolis Public Schools and *Writing the Outdoor Story* at the University of Wisconsin, the University of Minnesota, and the University of Florida.

Wrongway Santa is another delightful title in the long list of contributions to children's literature by Rae Oetting. Rae passed away before she saw the fruition of this work, but the publisher takes great pride in adding it to her extensive list of accomplishments.

about the illustrator

ART SHARDIN — His first name says it all. Art was born in Brooklyn, New York, and began his passionate pursuit of illustration, design, and art direction as soon as he learned to hold a pencil to a pad of paper . . . in his left hand, no less.

He attended New York City's prestigious High School of Art and Design and then completed his formal education at New York's equally renowned School of Visual Arts.

After a stint in the army, Art followed his talent from New York to Los Angeles, Miami, and finally, Atlanta. During that time he worked at some of the world's best ad agencies, including Doyle, Dane Bernbach, McCann-Erickson and BBDO. And along the way, he picked up just about every award the advertising industry accords to those of exceptional taste and talent.

A man of many disciplines, Art Shardin has also created greeting cards and posters, as well as commissioned paintings. A long-standing illustrator in advertising and public relations, he is proud of his first children's book assignment, *Wrongway Santa*.

A man who believes in "living the product," Art played traditional Christmas music throughout his house and festooned his studio in Yuletide decorations, including lights, for the entire time it took him to complete *Wrongway Santa* — which is most noteworthy when you consider that practically all the work was done during the summer when the temperature in Atlanta was well into the 90's!